Sue Bentley

Magic Ponies

Winter Wonderland

Illustrated by Angela Swan

PUFFIN

To Strawberry — pretty funster with attitude

PUFFIN BOOKS

Published by the Penguin Group
Penguin Books Ltd, 80 Strand, London WC2R 0RL, England
Penguin Group (USA) Inc., 375 Hudson Street, New York, New York 10014, USA
Penguin Group (Canada), 90 Eglinton Avenue East, Suite 700, Toronto, Ontario, Canada M4P 2Y3
(a division of Pearson Penguin Canada Inc.)
Penguin Ireland, 25 St Stephen's Green, Dublin 2, Ireland (a division of Penguin Books Ltd)
Penguin Group (Australia), 250 Camberwell Road, Camberwell, Victoria 3124, Australia
(a division of Pearson Australia Group Pty Ltd)
Penguin Books India Pvt Ltd, 11 Community Centre, Panchsheel Park, New Delhi – 110 017, India
Penguin Group (NZ), 67 Apollo Drive, Rosedale, North Shore 0632, New Zealand
(a division of Pearson New Zealand Ltd)
Penguin Books (South Africa) (Pty) Ltd, 24 Sturdee Avenue, Rosebank,
Johannesburg 2196, South Africa

Penguin Books Ltd, Registered Offices: 80 Strand, London WC2R 0RL, England

puffinbooks.com

First published 2009
1

Text copyright © Sue Bentley, 2009
Illustrations copyright © Angela Swan, 2009
All rights reserved

The moral right of the author and illustrator has been asserted

Set in Bembo
Made and printed in England by Clays Ltd, St Ives plc

British Library Cataloguing in Publication Data
A CIP catalogue record for this book is available from the British Library

ISBN: 978-0-141-32772-3

www.greenpenguin.co.uk

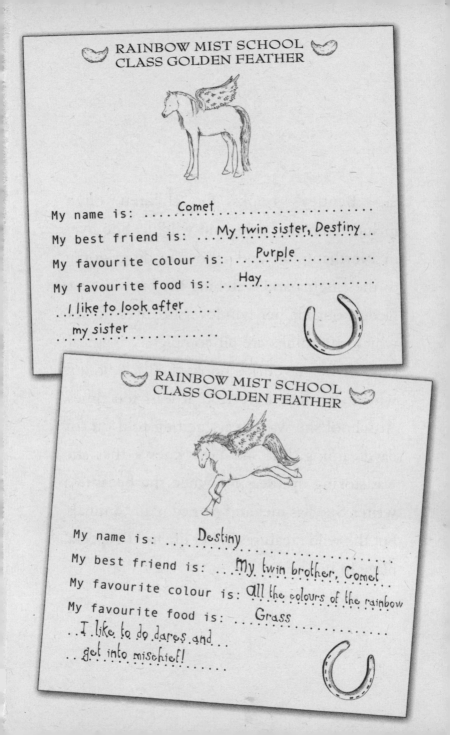

RAINBOW MIST SCHOOL
CLASS GOLDEN FEATHER

My name is: Comet

My best friend is: My twin sister, Destiny

My favourite colour is: Purple

My favourite food is: Hay

I like to look after my sister

RAINBOW MIST SCHOOL
CLASS GOLDEN FEATHER

My name is: Destiny

My best friend is: My twin brother, Comet

My favourite colour is: All the colours of the rainbow

My favourite food is: Grass

I like to do dares and get into mischief!

Sue Bentley's books for children often include animals, fairies and wildlife. She lives in Northampton and enjoys reading, going to the cinema and watching the birds on the feeders outside her window. She loves horses, which she thinks are all completely magical. One of her favourite books is *Black Beauty*, which she must have read at least ten times. At school she was always getting told off for daydreaming, but she now knows that she was storing up ideas for when she became a writer. Sue has met and owned many animals, but the wild creatures in her life hold a special place in her heart.

Prologue

Comet folded his gold-feathered wings as he galloped across the hillside on Rainbow Mist Island. The magic pony felt a stir of hope. Surely his twin sister had found her way home at last.

Destiny had been lost for so long.

Comet's cream-coloured coat and flowing gold mane and tail glistened in the moonlight. Overhead, stars pricked the midnight-blue sky. He sped onwards, past distant mountain tops that were wreathed in the multicoloured mist that gave Rainbow Mist Island its name.

Small stones struck deep violet sparks from his shining hooves. The magic pony slowed as he caught a movement. *There – at the cave entrance in that steep rock-face!*

Comet moved forward cautiously. He hoped it was another one of his Lightning Herd and not one of the dangerous dark horses. But he thought about how lonely he felt without his sister, and the magic pony decided to take a chance.

'Destiny?' he neighed softly.

An older horse with a wise expression stepped out from the cave. 'Your sister has not returned. But I am glad to see you again, my young friend,' he said in a deep velvety whinny.

'Blaze!' Comet bowed his head before the leader of the Lightning Herd.

Blaze's dark eyes softened as he saw Comet's disappointment. He picked his way across the rocks until he stood next to the magic pony.

'I do not think Destiny will come back, while she blames herself for losing our stone,' Blaze neighed softly.

The Stone of Power protected the Lightning Herd from the dark horses who wanted to steal their magic. The stone had become lost when Comet and Destiny were playing cloud-racing. Comet had found the stone, but Destiny had already fled.

'I wish I could find her and tell it is

safe to come home,' Comet said, sadly. 'But I do not know where she is.'

'The stone will help us!' Blaze struck the ground with one shining front hoof, and a fire-opal, glinting with many bright colours, appeared. 'Come closer, Comet.'

Comet's deep violet eyes glowed with eagerness as he did as Blaze urged. The stone grew larger and brighter and an image appeared in the rainbow depths. Comet saw Destiny galloping across a snow-covered field in a world far away.

He had to find her!

There was a bright flash of dazzling violet light and a rainbow mist swirled around Comet. Where the magnificent golden-winged pony had been there now stood a sturdy mouse-coloured Highland pony, with a darker-grey mane and tail.

'Go now, Comet!' Blaze said urgently. 'Use this disguise to find Destiny before the dark horses discover her!'

Comet's light-greyish-brown coat bloomed with violet sparks. He snorted softly as he felt the power building inside him. The rainbow mist swirled more thickly around him as it drew him in.

Chapter
ONE

'Yay! I totally love snow!' Preeti Nimesh exclaimed.

She stood looking out of her bedroom window, where someone seemed to have thrown a big soft white blanket over the garden during the night. The whole world looked fresh and new.

Huge soft flakes, like cotton-wool balls, were still falling. *Brilliant*, she thought, *the*

7

snow's going to last for ages!

Preeti ran out on to the landing. 'Mum! Dad! Grandma! Have you looked out of the window?' she called.

Her parents' bedroom opened and Mr Nimesh came out in his pyjamas looking sleepy-eyed. 'Do you know what time it is, Preeti? Where's the fire?' he asked, running a hand through his hair.

'There isn't one,' Preeti said, grinning. 'But I can't stay in bed any longer. Look!' She opened the landing curtains, so her dad could peer outside.

A shifting curtain of snow blurred the white landscape of front gardens and the street beyond. Usually there would be cars and buses going past. But this morning nothing was moving. Half-buried cars stood on many front drives.

'Goodness me!' her dad exclaimed.
'The snow must be at least twenty
centimetres thick. Your school's bound to
be closed and I think I'll be walking to
the surgery.'

Mr Nimesh was a doctor. Luckily, his
GP surgery was only a few streets away.

He went back into the bedroom and Preeti heard him talking to her mum.

'A day off school. Cool!' She clapped her hands in delight. She enjoyed all of her lessons. But if it came to school or playing in the snow with her friends – it was no contest.

Another bedroom door opened and a small boy exploded into the hall. His dark hair was shiny, like Preeti's. But where hers was long and straight, his was short and curly.

'Snow! Snow! Snow! Have you seen it?' Viren cried, whirling about and waving his arms like a human windmill.

'Yeah! Course I have!' Preeti said, rolling her eyes. 'Didn't you just hear me and Dad talking about it?'

At six years old, Viren was three years

younger than her and small for his age.
But he made up for it by having more
energy than a box of frogs. He finally
stopped spinning for long enough to pull
a face at her.

'I'm going to build a snow dinosaur
in the garden!' he exclaimed, crossing his
big brown eyes. 'You can help me if you
want.'

'I'm not sure what I'm doing yet,'
Preeti replied. 'I might phone Lisa and
Hayley, and ask them to come over.'

'Lisa and Hayley are dead boring!'
Viren sneered. 'All they talk about is
clothes and silly girlie stuff on TV.'

'No, they don't!' Preeti defended her
two best friends. 'You're just annoyed
because they don't want to hang out with
my extremely annoying little brother,' she

said with slow emphasis.

'Don't want to hang out with them
either!' Viren stuck out his tongue, darted
back into his bedroom and slammed the
door.

'Boys!' Preeti sighed as she went to
get dressed in warm clothes and boots.
Her grandma was making breakfast,
when Preeti came downstairs into the

big kitchen-diner. It was a big light room, with a table and chairs and comfy sofas set near patio doors that looked out on to the garden.

Sunetra Nimesh wore a pale green sari and her greying dark hair was pinned into a neat bun at the back of her head. Small stud earrings twinkled at her ears. She looked up with a warm smile. 'Good morning, darling.'

'Hi, Grandma!' Preeti sang out, sitting at the table and helping herself to the delicious freshly made chapattis. She loved it when Grandma made these for a special treat. They were much nicer than their normal breakfast cereal.

She was looking forward to the next few days. This was almost like having a winter holiday! As she ate, she began

making plans. Maybe she'd dig the old
sledge out of the barn, then she, Lisa and
Hayley could all go to the nearby park.
There was a big hill there and it would be
great fun to have races down the snow-
covered slope.

She decided that she'd phone them as
soon as she finished breakfast.

'I wonder what the weather forecast is.'
Grandma switched on the TV.

Preeti looked up as the announcer
began speaking.

'. . . heavy snow is expected for the
next two weeks. People are advised not
to travel unless it's absolutely necessary.
Many roads are impassable and most
schools and many businesses are closed.
There are no buses running at present . . .'

'Oh.' Preeti's shoulders drooped. Hayley

and Lisa both lived miles away, right across town. They weren't going to be able to get to her house. 'It's not going to be much fun staying off school if I'm all by myself,' she said glumly.

'It is lucky that you and Viren can play with each other,' Grandma said, pouring her a glass of milk.

Yeah, just great – not! Preeti thought. The last thing she felt like doing was babysitting her little brother.

'Good morning.' Mrs Nimesh greeted them both as she came in with Viren.

Preeti saw that her mum was wearing a tracksuit instead of the usual skirt and jacket she wore to the solicitor's office. She guessed that she'd decided to work from home today.

Preeti excused herself and stood up. 'I think I'll go to the barn and check on the pets. It's freezing outside and they might need extra bedding.'

'Aren't you glad that we haven't bought you that pony you wanted?' her mum commented. 'Imagine having to muck out in this awful weather.'

'I wouldn't mind,' Preeti said at once. She meant it too. She knew she'd do anything for a real pony of her own. She and Lisa and Hayley talked about them all the time.

'I'll help you!' Viren said, grabbing a

chapatti and leaping up.

Grandma put a hand on his arm. 'No, you will not. Stay there now. Eat,' she urged. 'Your sister can feed those rabbits and guinea pigs.'

Preeti grabbed her coat from the utility room and went outside. The air smelt cold and clean, with a chalky freshness. An icy wind was now blowing and cold snowflakes stung her face and stuck to her eyelashes. She wondered if Lisa and Hayley were missing her, as much as she was missing them.

Preeti pulled up her collar as she trudged through the deep snow. Her boots sank almost up to their tops as she picked her way slowly to the huge old barn at the bottom of the garden. Beyond it was a blurred white view of open fields and woods. Opening the barn door, she went inside.

A warm smell of clean animals met her. The far end of the barn housed her dad's lawnmower, workbench and gardening stuff. Three large hutches stood against one wall.

'Hi, guys!' Preeti said, bending down to talk to the dwarf rabbits and guinea pigs.

'Guess what. It's snowing outside! It's a
good thing you're all cosy in here.'

The little animals came snuffling up to
the wire mesh to greet her. Her favourites
were two handsome guinea pigs, called
Chandra and Surya. Surya had golden fur
that grew in swirly rosettes. And Chandra
had petal-soft, silver-tipped grey fur.

Preeti filled water bottles, tipped food
into bowls and replaced soiled bedding.
Luckily she had recently stocked up with
food. A friendly local farmer had sold
them a huge bale of straw and masses of
hay. So no matter how long the snow
lasted, she knew that the animals would
be warm and well fed.

She had just finished clearing up when
there was a bright flash of violet light
and a shimmering cloud appeared in the

centre of the barn. Preeti saw twinkling
crystal droplets forming on her coat
sleeves.

'Oh!' She narrowed her eyes as
she tried to see through the strange
multicoloured mist. Had some kind of
weird ice-storm blown into the barn?

As the mist began to fade, Preeti saw
that a pony was walking towards her.
It was sturdily built with a well-shaped
head, a pretty light-greyish-brown coat
and a darker-grey mane and tail.

'Can you help me, please?' it asked in a
velvety neigh.

Chapter
TWO

Preeti felt her mouth drop open as she stared at the pretty pony in complete shock. She must have been so amazed at seeing it just appear in their barn that she was imagining things. There was no way a pony could talk!

'Where did you just come from? However did you get in here?' she murmured to herself.

The pony flared its nostrils and lifted its head. 'I have just arrived here from far away,' it whinnied.

Preeti did a double take. 'Y–y–you really c–c–can talk? But . . . but how come?'

'All the other magical Lightning horses in my herd can talk,' the pony told her proudly. 'My name is Comet. What is yours?'

Preeti still couldn't believe this was really happening. It was like something out of a fairy tale. She felt like pinching herself to make sure she wasn't dreaming.

'I – I'm . . . um, Preeti Nimesh,' she found herself saying. 'I live here with my parents, my grandma and my little brother, Viren.'

Comet dipped his head in a formal bow and his dark-grey mane swung forward.

'I am honoured to meet you, Preeti.'

'Er . . . me too,' Preeti, said, wondering if she ought to curtsy or something. She settled for bowing her head in a jerky little movement. 'Did you say that you came from far away? Like a different town or something?'

'A lot further. I live in another world on Rainbow Mist Island, with my twin sister, Destiny.'

'Really? Cool! Is she outside in the snow?' Preeti asked, fascinated, about to go back into the garden and look for another talking pony.

Comet shook his head. 'Destiny is here in your world, but she is in hiding. She fled here after the Stone of Power was lost during a game of cloud-racing. This stone protects our Lightning Herd from the dark horses who want to steal our magic. I found it, but Destiny had already run away. I have come to find her and take her home.'

Preeti swallowed hard as she stared at the amazing pony, who, she noticed, had beautiful glowing deep violet eyes. He looked like a Highland pony she had seen in one of her magazines.

Everything Comet had told her

sounded so strange and magical. She was still having trouble taking it all in. But one thing, in particular, fascinated her.

'You say you were cloud-racing? But how...'

Comet's large eyes widened. 'Stand back please,' he snorted.

Preeti felt a warm tingling sensation flowing down to her fingertips as bright violet sparks bloomed in his mouse-coloured coat and more shimmering rainbow mist billowed around him. The sturdy Highland pony had gone and in its place was a pale-cream pony with a long flowing mane and tail that sparkled like spun gold thread. But it was the spreading, gold-feathered wings that sprang from his shoulders which stole Preeti's breath away.

'Oh!' she gasped in wonderment as she

gazed at the magnificent sight. She had never seen anything so beautiful in her entire life. 'Comet?'

'Yes, it is still me, Preeti. Do not be alarmed,' Comet said in a deep velvety neigh.

Before Preeti had time to get used to seeing Comet in his true form, there was another burst of violet sparkles and the multi-coloured mist dissolved into shimmering dust, revealing the sturdy grey-brown pony once more.

'Wow! That's a brilliant disguise. Can Destiny make herself look like you?'

Comet nodded, his tail twitching. 'But no disguise will help her if the dark horses find her. She has been far away from the Stone of Power for so long that they are able to see through her magic.

26

I must look for my sister. Will you help me?'

'Of course I will,' Preeti said at once, without thinking how difficult that could be.

She suddenly remembered the news announcement about how the weather had brought everything to a standstill. It had been bad enough making her way through the deep snow to get to the barn. Tramping through it for hours in search of a lost pony would be impossible.

She told Comet her worries. 'The snow's mega-thick outside and it's really hard to walk in it. Maybe I could ask Mum and Dad to help –' she began.

'No! I am sorry, but you cannot tell anyone about me or what I have told you,' Comet snorted, his eyes serious. 'You must promise me, Preeti.'

Preeti chewed at her bottom lip. She
felt disappointed that she couldn't tell
her parents about the amazing pony. She
was sure they would have kept his secret
– even if Viren definitely wouldn't have
been able to! But Comet was looking
at her with a mixture of complete trust
and confidence and she found herself
nodding.

'All right then,' she said hesitantly,
prepared to agree if it would keep Comet
and Destiny safe from their enemies.

'Thank you for keeping my secret.'
Comet gave a soft blow and reached
forward to gently nuzzle her coat sleeve.
'And do not worry. I have my magic to
help us when we search for Destiny.'

'That's . . . um, OK then,' Preeti said,
intrigued. She couldn't imagine what sort

of 'help' he meant, but she guessed it was going to be something really unusual.

As she reached up to stroke his satiny cheek, a proud smile spread across her face. A magic pony had chosen her to be his friend. How amazing was that?

Comet's ears swivelled and he turned his head towards the door. At the same time, Preeti heard a noise behind her. She spun round to see her little brother brushing snow off his coat as he stepped into the barn.

Catching sight of Preeti and Comet, Viren froze.

'Where did that pony come from?' he gasped, his big brown eyes like saucers.

Chapter
THREE

Preeti racked her brains as she tried to come up with something. What could she say to Viren? How could she explain Comet's presence?

'I found Comet in . . . um . . . the garden,' she began. 'He must have wandered in . . . from that empty field next to the road or something,' she went on, gaining confidence as she remembered that ponies were sometimes tethered there. 'Comet looked cold and hungry, so I decided to bring him into the barn.'

'He was pretty clever to come here, wasn't he?' Viren went up to Comet and stroked his nose. 'Poor thing. I bet you couldn't get to the grass, because of all the snow.' He turned back to Preeti. 'How come you know his name?'

'I don't,' Preeti fibbed. 'I called him Comet because . . . I've . . . erm, always liked that name.'

'I like it too. It suits him,' Viren decided. 'Comet can stay here, can't he? It's nice and warm and we can feed him on straw and stuff.'

'Ponies eat hay. Straw's just for their beds –' Preeti started explaining when Comet neighed eagerly.

'I would like to live in here, very much.
It is a safe place.' He pricked his ears as he
swept the barn with keen eyes.

Preeti did a double take. What was
Comet doing? He had just given himself
away in front of Viren!

But her little brother appeared not to
have noticed anything odd. It was very
strange.

Trying to gather her wits, she said,
'Well – I don't suppose anyone's going to
come looking for Comet until the roads
are clear. And he does need somewhere to
shelter from the –'

'So we *can* keep him? Cool!' Viren
interrupted. 'Great! I'll go and tell Mum
and Dad and Grandma. I'm going to get
a brush so I can groom him. We've got
a pet pony! We've got a pet pony!' he
chanted in an annoying sing-song voice,
jumping about.

Before Preeti could protest that Comet
was actually *her* friend and that he
definitely wasn't anyone's pet, especially
not Viren's, her little brother had slipped
outside. She went to the door and saw
him scuttling back to the house through
the tracks she'd made earlier.

'I'm going to tell everyone about Comet. I can't wait to see the looks on their faces!' he shouted over his shoulder to her.

Preeti gave a sigh and tried not to feel too disappointed. She'd been really excited about doing that herself. Even if she could only say that Comet was a normal pony who had turned up looking for food and shelter.

She turned back to the magic pony. 'Now Viren's decided that you belong to both of us, we'll never get rid of him. He'll be trailing around with us all the time.'

'Viren seems like a nice little boy,' Comet neighed.

'But he can be a real pest,' Preeti said, shaking her head slowly. 'Everyone lets him do just what he wants. So he's totally spoilt.' But something else was bothering her. 'How come he didn't seem to hear you speak to me just now?'

Comet wrinkled his lips in amusement. 'I used my magic so that only you will be able to see and hear me. To anyone else I will seem like a normal pony.'

'Really?' Preeti felt herself cheering up.

Viren might have laid claim to Comet, but only she had been trusted with her new friend's wonderful secret!

'Comet had better live in our barn until the weather breaks and we can find out who owns him,' Mrs Nimesh was saying as Preeti came back into the house. 'I know it's not an ideal stable, but it'll only be for a short time.' She smiled at her daughter. 'It looks like you've a pony to take care of, after all, Preeti!'

'Yay! Isn't it brilliant?' Preeti felt her grin stretch from ear to ear.

'And I have. Comet's half mine!' Viren insisted.

Preeti wisely kept silent.

Her mum went to make a quick phone call to the local pet centre and leave their address and phone number, in case Comet's owner turned up.

Preeti was totally confident that no one was going to claim her secret magical friend.

'We're keeping the pony. We're keeping the pony!' Viren pretended to be riding round the kitchen. Clicking his tongue, he made clopping noises as he galloped out of the kitchen and thudded up the stairs.

Preeti decided to go back down to the barn to tell Comet the good news about him being allowed to stay. Besides, she wanted to settle him in properly. She was halfway down the garden when she heard a familiar voice.

'Wait for me! I'm coming too. I want to help!' Viren insisted.

'OK then, but you have to do as I say,' she told him.

He frowned. 'Why?'

'Because I'm older and I know how to look after ponies,' Preeti said firmly. 'Deal?'

Viren groaned, but when he saw that she was serious, he shrugged. 'Deal.'

Comet looked up as they came in. 'Greetings, Preeti. Greetings, Viren,' he snorted.

'Hi, Comet!' Viren sang out, rushing straight over to stroke him.

Preeti smiled at Comet. 'We've come to make you a comfortable stable.'

She showed Viren how to spread a thick layer of straw to make a cosy bed.

'Easy-peasy!' He gathered armfuls of straw, but he dropped more than half of it and left wisps and clumps all over the floor.

Preeti decided that it was easier to just let him get on with it and then clear up afterwards. She knew from experience that her brother would get stroppy if she pointed out that he was making a mess.

'Right. Finished!' Viren said proudly a few minutes later. He dusted off his hands. 'I'm going to build a snowman now! Come and help me, Preeti.'

'I still have to finish up in here. You make a start and I'll follow you in a minute,' she said.

'Well, hurry up then.'

Once her brother had gone outside, Preeti filled a bucket with water and then

found some old netting and managed to
rig up a makeshift hay net.

Comet nibbled at the hay with his
strong young teeth. 'It is very warm and
safe here. Thank you,' he whinnied.

'You're welcome!' Preeti smiled, pleased
that Comet liked his cosy new stable.

'Preeti! Where are you?' Viren bawled
impatiently from the garden. 'I'm getting
fed up by myself.'

'I'm just clearing up!' Preeti called to
him. She sighed. *What a mess!*

She was just about to start tackling it,
when she felt a strange tingling sensation
flowing down to the ends of her fingers.
Bright violet sparks ignited in Comet's
silky mouse-brown coat and his dark-grey
mane crackled with tiny lightning bolts
of power.

Preeti's eyes widened. Something very strange was about to happen.

She watched in amazement as every last scrap of the scattered straw twitched up into the air. *Swoosh! Crackle!* It swirled around for a few seconds, before gathering together and forming the shape of a large straw robot. *Rustle!* He marched across the barn to where the straw bales were stored and jumped on top of them.

With a soft whispering sound, the straw robot collapsed into a neat heap, just as every last bright spark faded from Comet's coat.

'Wow! That was amazing!' Preeti said. 'It would have taken me ages to clear that lot up. Thanks, Comet.'

'You are welcome. Now you can go and have fun in the snow too.' Comet leaned forward to push his satiny nose into her hands.

Preeti's heart melted as the magic pony huffed warm grass-scented breath over her fingers. She felt a surge of fondness for him. Comet hadn't been here for long, but she already loved him to bits.

Chapter
FOUR

As Preeti made her way back up the garden, it finally stopped snowing. The sky was milk-white above the rooftops.

Viren was on the small lawn outside the sitting-room window. He was puffing and panting as he piled armfuls of snow into a big mound.

'You've been ages,' he complained, moodily. 'I bet you wanted to stay there

with Comet, so you had him all to
yourself. He's mine too, you know!'

'Actually, I was clearing up the mess
you made!' Preeti exclaimed. She bit
back an even ruder reply, as she silently
counted to ten. 'Never mind. Let's build
this snowman,' she said more calmly, as
she bent down to scoop up some snow.

Thump! A snowball hit her on the arm.

'What a shot!' Viren crowed.

'Hey!' Grinning, Preeti threw one back
at him.

Suddenly, they were pelting each other with snowballs. In all the fun of the fight, Preeti forgot for a while to be cross with her brother. Her breath was steaming out in the cold air and her cheeks began to glow.

'Truce!' she gasped finally, as another snowball hit her on the head and powdery snow dribbled inside her coat collar. 'We'd better stop now or we'll never get this snowman built!'

'OK,' Viren agreed. 'But I won!' His cheeks were flushed too and his dark eyes shone mischievously.

'If you say so,' Preeti said.

'I do!' he shot back, having the last word.

They made a big pile of snow and patted it into shape. Soon they had the snowman's body. Preeti showed her little brother how to roll a snowball around, so that it gathered snow, and it soon grew to the right shape and size for a head.

'Shall we give him a face?' she asked.

'Not yet,' Viren said, his eyes sparkling. 'We have to make some legs.'

'Legs?' Preeti raised her eyebrows; then she remembered his earlier plan to make a snow dinosaur.

They made four stumpy legs and fixed them on, so they stuck straight out from the snowman's body. They looked rather odd, but Viren nodded in satisfaction. He began forming two small triangular ears on the top of the head and shaping the face into a longish muzzle.

'That's the funniest looking dinosaur I've ever seen!' Preeti said, starting to laugh.

Viren frowned. 'It's not a dinosaur.
Can't you tell what it is?'

'Give me a clue!' Preeti said, putting
her head on one side.

'Just a minute.' Viren went and
scrabbled in the snow beneath a small
tree and then returned with a handful
of twigs. He jabbed a clump of them
between the lumpy ears and placed the

rest of them in a line that marched down
the back of the neck.

'Now can you tell what it is?' he asked.

'A snow alien?' Preeti spluttered.

Viren scowled with annoyance. He
stuck his hands on his hips. 'No, you great
wally. It's a snow pony! Ob-viously!'

'Ob-viously – not!' Preeti replied – it
looked a very odd pony to her.

'I've made a friend for Comet. I'm
going to tell him,' Viren said, heading
back towards the barn.

'I'll come with you,' Preeti said,
breathing on her gloves to warm her cold
fingers. 'Then I think we should go and
get some hot chocolate. I'm freezing.'

'OK. Maybe Comet's cold too. We
could bring him some hot chocolate.'

'Ponies only drink water,' she told him,

not really concentrating. 'And he'll be
fine in the barn. He said that he likes it
there, because it's cosy and warm.'

'How come Comet told you that?'
Viren scoffed. 'Ponies can't talk!'

'Um . . . no, of course they can't. I was
. . . erm, just thinking that's what he'd say
if he *could* talk,' Preeti said hastily, realizing
that she was going to have be more
careful about keeping Comet's secret.

'It's so cool having a pony to look after,'
Viren declared excitedly. I'm going to
spend every moment I can out here with
Comet. I might bring my sleeping bag
out so I can sit and read to him. And I
could . . .'

Preeti's heart sank as Viren rattled on.
The way her little brother was taking
over completely was mega-annoying and

presented her with a big problem.

'I can't see how I'm going to slip away by myself so we can search for Destiny,' she whispered to Comet. 'He's even talking about camping out in the barn!'

Comet's deep violet eyes twinkled and he swished his grey tail. 'I believe in you, Preeti. I know you will think of a way,' he neighed confidently.

Chapter
FIVE

It began snowing again as evening fell and soon covered the tracks Preeti and Viren had made down the garden earlier. The news on TV showed pictures of people stranded on motorways and planes unable to take off from airports. Everything was at a standstill.

'The trouble is, we're not used to this weather in this country,' Mrs Nimesh said, switching channels with the remote controller. 'If we were, there'd be special measures in place to deal with it, like snowploughs to clear the main roads.'

Grandma glanced out of the sitting-room window at the snow pony on the lawn. It seemed to glow faintly in the moonlight. 'He is rather splendid. He could be there for a long time in this freezing weather,' she commented.

Preeti was curled up in a chair, reading

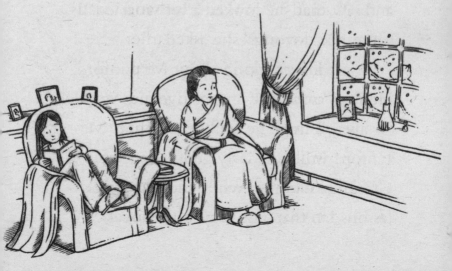

a book of pony stories. She loved the
feeling of being warm and cosy inside
the house when everything was white
and frozen outside. Comet was safe in
the barn and there would be no school
for ages, so she could spend loads of time
with him.

If only she could think of a way
of distracting Viren for a few hours,
everything would be perfect.

She looked up to smile at her grandma
and saw that she looked a bit worried. 'Is
something wrong?' she asked.

'I was just thinking about Mr Linford.
He lives alone and his relatives are very
far away. I hope he will be all right.' Mr
Linford was an elderly gentleman who
Grandma had met while she was giving
lessons in Asian cookery at the local

community centre. They often met for a
chat and a cup of tea.

'Does he live very far away?' Preeti
asked.

'No. It is only three minutes away by
car. But, of course, I cannot drive to see
him.'

'Why don't you walk there and visit
him?' Preeti suggested. She had a sudden
brainwave. 'Maybe Viren will go with
you.'

Grandma smiled. 'That is a kind
thought. I think I will phone Mr Linford
now.' She left the room and Preeti soon
heard her talking to her friend.

'How is he?' she asked, when her
grandma returned a few minutes later.

'Mr Linford said he is fine for now,'
Grandma told her. 'But he is rather

worried that he cannot get out of his house to get to the shops for milk and bread. Perhaps we could visit him, in a day or two, and take him some groceries?'

Mr Nimesh looked up from where he sat reading his newspaper. 'The pavements are very icy, Mother. Please take great care if you go out walking.'

Grandma nodded worriedly. 'Ice is a problem. Well, perhaps this cold spell will not last. Those TV weathermen do not know everything.' She shook her head slowly as she went into the kitchen.

Preeti watched her go. She hadn't really thought about the problems that snow could bring. She realized now that this weather wasn't fun for everyone, especially older people.

She read for a bit longer and then

stifled a yawn as she closed her book. It
was getting late and she decided to go
and see Comet before she went upstairs
to bed. Viren had left the room a little
while ago and she thought she had heard
him going upstairs. He was probably
already in bed, asleep.

But the moment Preeti went into the
garden, she spotted the fresh tracks in the
snow that led to the barn.

Viren hadn't gone to bed at all. He had sneaked out again to see Comet. She couldn't suppress a prickle of resentment. It was starting to look as if she'd never be alone with Comet.

Then she had an idea. There was only one thing for it.

Preeti woke with a start, to find the bedroom still dark and the house silent.

She dressed quickly, being extra careful not to make any noise, and crept downstairs. Grabbing the nearest coat, she threw it on and then thrust her feet into a pair of worn old boots, before tiptoeing outside.

The bright moonlight cast midnight-blue shadows across the snow and made it easy to see as she went down to the barn.

Comet gave a soft neigh of welcome as she slipped inside. 'You are alone?'

'Yes, at last! Hi, Comet.' Preeti reached up to stroke his silky cheek. 'We've got lots of time to go out looking for Destiny before everyone wakes up! Let's go!'

'Thank you. Climb on to my back, Preeti.' Comet tossed his head with eagerness, his eyes flashing.

Preeti nervously climbed up and sat astride him. It had been ages since her last riding lesson and, anyway, she wasn't used to riding bareback. But the moment she twined her hands in his thick grey mane, Comet's warm magic seemed to spread around her and she felt completely safe and secure.

Comet moved forward and in two strides reached the closed barn door.

'Wait! I'll open it . . .' Preeti began.

Then she gasped as, with a flash of
bright violet sparks, Comet gave a mighty
leap and floated *through* the door in a
swoosh of glittering mist, which left
the door unchanged. They were soon
galloping across the snow, the magic
pony's shining hooves barely brushing the
white surface and leaving no tracks.

Chapter
SIX

Preeti laughed aloud with delight as they sped along in the silver moonlight, with snowflakes gently falling around them. Excitement raced through her. Comet was amazing to ride, so smooth and thrilling. His magic surrounded them and however fast they raced along she felt perfectly safe.

The magic pony's head turned left and

right as he rushed onwards. His keen eyes were searching for any sign that Destiny had come this way.

'Hold tight!' Comet warned.

He flashed over silent roads in the blink of an eye, and shops and houses passed by in a blur. They shot past factories and buildings until they came to the edge of town. An expanse of snow-covered fields stretched ahead of them.

'Look!' Preeti cried after a while, pointing to a field with a shelter at one end. Tractor marks led across the snow to a bale of hay, which four hardy little ponies with thick winter coats were eating. 'Maybe Destiny is disguised as one of those.'

Comet checked his stride and slowed as he cantered over to investigate. But none

of the little group was Destiny. He trotted
away sadly.

'I hope Destiny is hiding somewhere
safe,' Comet nickered, his head drooping.
'The dark horses will steal her magic if
they can.'

Preeti could see that he was badly
missing his twin sister. 'We'll come out
looking every night,' she promised.
'Maybe it will be easier to find her with
no people or cars about. Everywhere is

deserted because of the snow.'

'That is true.' Comet gave a long soft blow as he looked around with renewed interest. His breath hung in the freezing air like twinkling clouds of steam.

Slowing his stride, he moved at a gentler pace. Preeti rose to the trot as they checked out some woods. Soon they emerged opposite a deep railway cutting before moving onwards again. But they didn't see any other ponies.

Preeti noticed a faint rosy light beginning to wash across the sky. Dawn was approaching.

'I think we'd better head for home. Grandma gets up really early,' she said reluctantly.

'Very well.' Comet took a circular route that eventually brought them back across the fields and to the dual carriageway leading into town.

It began to snow more heavily, making it difficult to see far ahead. Preeti shivered, wishing now that she'd taken the time to put on her warmest coat with the fake-fur trimmed hood and her newest boots.

The coat she'd picked up in a hurry was a very light summer one.

'You are cold,' Comet whickered.

Preeti felt a faint tingling feeling in her fingertips as Comet's mane twinkled with tiny violet sparkles. A clear bubble spread round her, keeping her warm and dry. The snowflakes melted as they touched the bubble's surface, so she could also see where they were going.

'That's much better. Thanks, Comet.' Suddenly, Preeti caught a movement from the corner of her eye. 'Hold on. Look! Over there. In that ditch.'

'Is it Destiny?' Comet neighed urgently, rocking on to his back legs as he halted.

Preeti clung on tight. Just beyond the roadside, the ground sloped sharply away. Comet stood looking down into the ditch, which seemed to be filled by a big lumpy snowdrift. But there was no pony sheltering there.

'What's that?' Preeti frowned, puzzled, staring at the pile of snow. 'It looks like a bit of door and back window.' Her eyes widened in shock. 'Oh my goodness! There's a car under there! And I think someone's inside it!'

Chapter
SEVEN

'We have to help!' Preeti cried.

Comet nodded. 'Lean against me. We will climb down together.'

Quickly dismounting, Preeti put one arm round Comet's neck and braced herself against his strong shoulder as they slid and stumbled down the deep bank until they reached the ditch.

Luckily the car seemed to have just slid

down and landed the right way up. The front of it was sloping slightly downwards.

Preeti began frantically trying to clear snow from the side windows. 'If I can just brush some of this away, we'll be able to see inside the car!' But in just seconds her hands were numb with cold.

'I will help,' Comet neighed beside her.

Preeti felt another warm prickling sensation flowing to the ends of her fingers as he huffed out a sparkly breath that twinkled with thousands of tiny rainbow stars. The glittering mist swirled around the car for a few seconds and swept up the entire covering of snow, which then fell far away in the field beyond.

As the car was revealed, Preeti saw two faces looking out at them. It was a

woman and a little girl who looked about
Viren's age. They were huddled together
under layers of coats as they tried to keep
warm.

'Are you OK?' Preeti called, tapping on
the window.

The woman nodded. She leaned
over to speak to her through the closed
window. 'We're not hurt, just a bit cold,'
she shouted. 'I phoned for help on my

mobile. We've been waiting here for hours. I think a big lorry or something went past a while back, but it didn't see us. I didn't dare leave Emily and go up to the road to flag it down. I stayed here and tried to keep us both warm.'

'That was the best thing to do,' Comet whinnied to Preeti.

The woman in the car did a double take as she heard pony noises. She peered over Preeti's shoulder and seemed to see Comet for the first time in the thick swirling snow. 'Is that your pony? But . . . how come . . .? What . . .?'

Preeti thought quickly. 'We're . . . erm . . . helping the . . . rescue team,' she said vaguely. 'Don't worry. Help will soon be here.'

The woman nodded gratefully. 'We

have a chance of being seen, now that you've cleared the snow away, though I don't know how you did it. And it's strange, but it feels a lot warmer in here now.'

Preeti smiled with relief when a moment later she saw Comet prick up his ears. Seconds later, Preeti heard it too. The chugging rumble of a snowplough. Powerful searchlights penetrated the blinding snow as the big lorry appeared round a bend.

The woman and her daughter, Emily, would be fine now but she and Comet had to leave before anyone else knew that they'd been there. She didn't want her mum and dad finding out about her midnight ride.

Comet leaned forward to gently snuffle

her hair. 'We must leave now,' he neighed. The sky was much lighter and the sound of the lorry was getting closer.

Preeti leaned close to the window to speak to the woman one final time. 'We have to go now. Bye!' she called, backing away.

'Wait! How can I thank you . . .?' the woman shouted.

But her voice faded as Preeti turned and held on to Comet again, and they climbed out of the ditch. Once back on the road, she mounted again.

'Well done, Comet!' she praised.

Bending forward, she heard the wind whistling past them outside the magical bubble as Comet went flat out. The blizzard raged on, but she was safe and warm. In the early morning light, the

swirling snowflakes were tinted pale
apricot and gold. Once again, Preeti felt
the heart-stopping thrill of riding the
magic pony. And she knew she would
remember this amazing night for the rest
of her life.

Back at the barn, she rubbed Comet
down and made sure he had fresh water

and hay. 'You were brilliant tonight, Comet!' she told him, stroking his velvety nose. 'Those people in the car will be rescued because of you.'

His deep violet eyes gleamed. 'I am glad I could help.'

'You deserve a rest. You've been riding hard,' she said fondly, stranding his mane through her fingers.

'I would gallop all day without a rest, if it meant I would find Destiny,' he told her, blowing out a long breath through his flared nostrils. 'You are lucky that your little brother is safe and here with you.'

Preeti hadn't thought about it like that. Viren was such a pest that she sometimes wished she was an only child, but she did love him really.

'I know you miss Destiny a lot,' she

said gently. She put her arms round his neck and laid her cheek against his warm silky coat. 'I wish we could find her too. And then maybe you could both live here with me? I could ask Mum and Dad if we could make part of the barn into a proper stable.'

Comet shook his head slowly. 'I am afraid that is not possible. Destiny and I must go back to our Lightning Herd on Rainbow Mist Island.'

'Oh,' Preeti sighed. She supposed she knew that really, but she didn't want to believe it. It was just too painful to think of her special friend leaving. She decided to push it to the back of her mind.

'I'll see you later,' she said, as she went out and closed the barn door behind her.

From now on, she was going to

make sure that she enjoyed every single moment spent with Comet.

Chapter
EIGHT

'It is strange to think that we will celebrate *Holi* in a few days,' Grandma commented the following day. She was in the kitchen, making coconut sweets. 'Who would think it would snow so heavily in March?'

'I know, it doesn't feel like we should be celebrating the coming of spring,' Preeti replied. She was helping to make

the delicious sweets they usually gave
away as gifts when visiting friends and
relatives.

Mrs Nimesh came in from her office
to have a coffee break. 'You two look
busy,' she said, smiling, looking at the trays
of colourful treats. 'So many? Who will
eat them all? I think it might be a rather
quiet *Holi* this year.'

Preeti felt disappointed, as she thought

her mum could be right. The snow was stopping everyone from travelling.

She loved it when everyone gathered together at festival times. *Holi* was particularly good fun because it was associated with Lord Krishna, who was famous for mischief-making and playing tricks on his friends. It was a time for everyone to do the same. People wore their oldest clothes and threw brightly coloured powders at each other.

Viren enjoyed it especially, because he was allowed to get really messy without being told off! But this year it looked as if their family would be celebrating alone because of the dangerously icy roads.

'Couldn't we have a party here?' Preeti pleaded, looking at her mum. 'Some of our friends live close enough to walk. We

could make a big bonfire on the snow.
Dad's got lots of dry wood in the barn.
It would be good fun and we could keep
warm playing games and dancing.'

Her mum looked thoughtful. 'It
would mean a lot of work, cooking and
preparing party food.'

'I'll help!' Preeti offered at once.

Mrs Nimesh nodded. 'All right. Why
not? I will go and make some phone calls,
right away.'

'Yay!' Preeti cried delightedly.

Viren wandered in playing a computer
game. It was making twittering and
popping noises as he pressed the buttons
with his thumbs. He pinched a few of the
cooling coconut squares, and popped a
piece in his mouth.

'Mmm. You make the best sweets in the

whole world, Grandma!' he exclaimed, rubbing his tummy.

'You cheeky boy! You will not get round me like that!' Grandma ruffled her grandson's curly dark hair, but she was smiling with pleasure. 'But that's enough now or you will not eat your lunch,' she scolded fondly.

Viren turned to Preeti. 'Who's Mum phoning?' Preeti told him about the party they were planning. 'Cool! A snow-party. Comet can come too. We'll powder him with all different colours. He'll love *Holi*!' Plonking himself on the sofa at the far end of the kitchen-diner, Viren switched on the TV.

Preeti was rolling sweet mixture into small balls, when she heard the newsreader's voice floating towards her.

'. . . a woman who was rescued in the
early hours of yesterday morning after
her car skidded into a ditch has reported
a mysterious ghostly sighting of a girl and
a pony. Apparently the girl spoke to her.
The driver of a snowplough also glimpsed
them briefly in his headlights, before the
girl and her pony disappeared without
trace. If anyone has any information . . .'

'Oh no!' Preeti murmured under

her breath. She felt herself growing hot and was sure her face must have been bright red. 'I have to go and . . . erm . . . do something in the barn,' she burbled hastily, washing her sticky hands. 'See you later!' she called over her shoulder as she high-tailed it out of the kitchen.

Grandma and Viren didn't respond. They were glued to the TV, spellbound by the story of the ghostly girl and her pony.

'Phew! I didn't expect to hear about us on the news!' Preeti said to Comet. She had removed his soiled bedding and spread fresh straw and was now giving the guinea pigs some bits of cucumber for a treat. Chandra and Surya were making excited grunting noises, as they snuffled and licked cucumber juice from her

fingers. 'It's a good thing that woman and
the snowplough driver didn't get a proper
look at us or I'd be in deep trouble with
Mum and Dad now!'

With Comet looking after her, Preeti
knew she couldn't have been in safer
hands. But her parents wouldn't see it like
that. She didn't fancy trying to explain
what she was doing riding about at night.

Comet's grey mane swung forward as
he nodded in agreement. 'When we go
out looking for Destiny again, I will use
my magic to make us both invisible.'

'You can do that? Wow! That's *so* cool!
Then I needn't worry about anyone
seeing us.'

It had been so amazing to ride Comet.
She had loved their exciting snowy
adventure. 'I'd like to go out with you

again right now,' she said, although she knew it was far too risky, especially with Viren likely to pop his head into the barn at any moment. 'Though I'd better wait and slip out when everyone's asleep, like last night.'

But by a stroke of luck, Preeti found herself with time on her hands that afternoon. Grandma was walking over to visit her friend, Mr Linford, and Mum and Viren had gone with her. Her dad was at the surgery, so the house was empty for once.

'I pretended I had some homework to do,' she told Comet. 'So I could stay here. Now we can go out looking for Destiny.'

'Thank you, Preeti.' Comet's eyes flashed and he pawed the floor with one front hoof. 'Climb on to my back again.'

Preeti didn't need telling twice. As they galloped away from the barn, she showed him the way to a different part of town to last time. Once again, Comet's shining hooves skimmed the surface of the snow and their invisible passing left no trail.

Gritter lorries had been busy and traffic was beginning to move very slowly on the main road. Preeti saw lots of snow-covered cars left on drives and parked along kerbs. Ice and snow blocked all the side roads.

'There's a park just over there with lots of places where Destiny might hide,' Preeti said, pointing.

Comet pricked his ears hopefully.

As they drew closer they could hear shouts and laughter. About thirty kids of all ages were playing in the snow. More of

them were sledging down a steep hill.

Preeti and Comet rode between the trees and snow-covered bushes, keeping a sharp eye out for any signs of a pony. At first, Preeti found it strange that no one paid them any attention, but she soon got used to it.

Being invisible was great fun!

They investigated an area with clipped hedges, but found nothing. Comet snorted and they rode on towards a large frozen lake.

Ducks and geese waddled on the surface and noisy seagulls wheeled overhead. A forest of tall dried reeds stuck up through the snow along a stretch of the lakeside, providing enough cover for a lost pony. But once again they had no luck.

Galloping away from the park, Comet headed towards a shopping centre.

'Let's try over there,' Preeti said, squeezing him on, as she pointed to a superstore with a large car park. 'Maybe it would be warmer behind the store. A pony could find shelter there.'

Comet nodded, flicking up his tail with eagerness.

But he had barely begun to cross the snow-covered car park when Preeti felt him stiffen. As her magic pony friend stopped and leaned down to look at the ground, she looked down too.

In front of them both and stretching all the way across the car park was a faint line of softly glowing violet hoof-prints.

'Destiny! She came this way!' Comet neighed excitedly.

Preeti felt a pang. Did that mean her friend was leaving right now? 'Are . . . are you going follow her?' she asked anxiously.

Comet shook his head. 'No. There is no point. This trail is not fresh. But it proves that Destiny was here. She cannot be too far away. When she is very close, I will be able to hear her hoof-beats.'

'Will I be able to hear them too?' Preeti asked.

'Yes. But only if you are riding me, or

we are together,' he explained in a soft neigh. 'And I may have to leave suddenly, without saying goodbye, to catch up with her.'

Preeti bit her lip during this reminder that Comet could not stay with her forever. She swallowed hard as tears threatened to well up, knowing that she would never be ready to lose her special magic friend.

Chapter
NINE

After searching for a while longer, with
no more signs of Destiny, Preeti and
Comet turned towards home. Preeti
wasn't sure how long Grandma, Mum and
Viren would stay at Mr Linford's house,
and she hoped they would get back
before they returned.

On the way, they cut through some
narrow lanes and alleyways and finally

emerged at the far side of the park, a short way from the frozen lake. A group of people were on the shore. As they drew closer, shouts rang out.

'A little boy's fallen through the ice!' a girl cried.

Preeti tightened her hands on Comet's mane and looked towards the commotion. She had a bad feeling about this. More people were running towards the lake, where a tiny shape out on the ice was waving its arms about.

As the magic pony checked his stride, Preeti frowned. There was something familiar about that figure. Then her heart missed a beat.

'It's Viren!' she gasped.

Whatever was her little brother doing here?

Comet didn't hesitate. 'Hold tight!'

He launched himself into the air in
a mighty leap. Seconds later he landed
lightly on the lake's frozen surface, in the
centre of the reed bed. Half a metre away,
Viren's head and shoulders were sticking
up through a hole in the ice as he tried to
pull himself out.

Quickly dismounting, Preeti crawled
forward and knelt at the edge of the reeds.

'Hang on, Viren!' she gasped.

'Preeti? Is that you?' His frightened
dark eyes widened in shock as he looked

around, trying to see where her voice had
come from. 'Where . . . where are you?' he
gulped, his teeth chattering.

Preeti remembered that she and Comet
were still invisible. What was she to
do? How could she explain her sudden
appearance? There was no blizzard to hide
them this time. She felt torn. She had to
help her brother, but she had promised to
keep Comet's secret.

Preeti made up her mind.

'Comet! Make me visible please!' she
whispered.

The magic pony's wise eyes gleamed.
'Very well.'

Preeti felt the familiar warm tingling
feeling flow down her fingers and saw
bright sparks igniting in Comet's coat as
a shimmering multicoloured mist swirled

around them. The magical rainbow
fog spread out across the lake's surface,
making the ice safe and hiding them from
the people on the shore.

Preeti lay down and inched herself
forward on to the thicker ice. 'Don't
worry! I'm here!' she called to Viren.

His face crumpled with relief. 'Preeti!'

Almost there! Preeti kicked out
strongly with her feet and skidded
towards him. Yes! Her fingers closed on
a wet sleeve. 'Got you!'

She took a firm hold, pulled with all
her strength and hauled Viren out. He
collapsed in a wet heap on to the ice
beside her.

For a moment she lay there, panting.
Viren was shivering badly.

A magical fleecy blanket of

shimmering rainbow mist settled warmly
around them both. 'Quickly, while he is
still confused. Lift him on to my back,'
Comet neighed softly.

Preeti was worried that Viren would
be too heavy for her. But as she scooped
him up in her arms, she found that he
was as light as a feather, and she mounted

Comet easily.

With a burst of violet sparkles, Comet made them all invisible before he sprang into the air. His giant leap carried them high above the frozen lake. Then, landing on the shore, he bore them home at the speed of light.

Preeti hardly had time to catch her breath before she found herself inside the warm barn. Moments later, she was standing beside Comet, looking down at Viren, who lay on the clean straw.

Her brother sat up, rubbing his eyes as if he was waking from a dream. 'What . . . what just happened?' Viren blinked up at her in surprise. 'I . . . I don't get it. How did I get back here?'

'I managed to grab you and pull you out of the water. You were in a bit of a

daze, but you managed to walk home
with me,' Preeti improvised quickly. 'It
was lucky I was at the park and saw you
fall through the ice. What were you doing
there anyway? You know you're not
allowed to go off by yourself. If Mum and
Dad find out about this, you're toast!'

Viren's face clouded. 'You won't tell
them, will you?' he pleaded.

'I haven't decided yet. Why *were* you
at the park, anyway?' she asked him.

Viren hung his head and looked
sorry for himself. 'After I got back from
Grandma's friend's house, I came to see
Comet. But he wasn't in the barn!
When I couldn't find you either, I went
to look for him by myself. I thought he
might go to the park because there was
grass there to eat.'

Preeti nodded. It kind of made sense.

She felt a stir of guilt. This was partly
her fault. She could have invited Viren
to help her look after Comet, instead of
always trying to avoid him. And maybe
if she and Comet had come back earlier,
none of this would have happened. Viren
had been quite brave to try to find the
lost pony all by himself.

'What about you? Why were you
there?' Viren demanded. 'I thought
you were supposed to be doing your
homework.'

'I was. But I finished it. So I went for a
walk,' Preeti fibbed. 'Anyway, never mind
that. The main thing is that you're OK
now.'

Viren didn't challenge her. He gave
a subdued nod and then stood up and

brushed himself down. A grin spread over his face. 'Comet came back, didn't he? So that's all right! He likes living here with us!' Viren reached up to put both arms round Comet's neck and buried his face against the warm grey-brown skin.

The magic pony swung his head down and gently butted the little boy's arm.

'Yes. I like it here,' he neighed softly, although Viren only heard normal pony noises.

Preeti waited until Viren had finished cuddling Comet. She was pleased to see that the colour had come back to her brother's face and that he seemed none the worse for his frightening experience on the ice.

'I think you should go and get out of those wet clothes before Mum starts asking awkward questions, don't you?' she suggested gently.

'OK!' Viren didn't need telling twice. 'Thanks for not snitching, sis!' He rushed at her and gave her a swift damp hug before running out.

Preeti stared after him. A smile curved her lips. Viren could be annoying

sometimes, but he could be sweet too.
Besides, he was the only brother she had.

Chapter
NINE

At last it was *Holi* Eve. The evening was clear and very cold and still.

A colourful feast was spread out in the house. Preeti's mouth watered at all the delicious smells. She stood looking into the garden, where she could see Viren and her dad putting the finishing touches to the bonfire.

Her brother saw her looking and

waved. Preeti smiled and waved back.
They had been getting on better since
what had happened in the park.

   She decided to quickly slip down to
the barn. This might be the only chance
she got to spend a few moments alone
with Comet this evening. She helped
herself to a big rosy apple from the fruit
bowl in the kitchen. After quickly slicing
it, she slipped it into her pocket.

Earlier, she had pushed candles into the snow to encircle the small lawn close to the house. As she walked past, their light flickered on to the snow pony that she and Viren had made over a week ago.

Grandma was right. In this freezing weather, it had lasted well.

She reached the barn and went inside to where the magic pony was waiting. At the sight of him, a warm glow spread through her. He was her special secret and she'd never tell anyone about him.

'Greetings, Preeti,' Comet whinnied, turning to look at her.

She smiled as she reached up to stroke him in the sensitive place between his eyes. 'I've got something for you.' She took out the apple and fed it to him slice by slice.

Comet crunched it up in his strong teeth. 'Delicious.'

'Our friends and relatives will be here soon,' she told him. 'I can't wait for them to see you. In a little while we'll say prayers and light the fire. Then we throw offering of coconuts, popcorn and rice into the flames. You'll love celebrating *Holi* with us!'

Comet nodded, his deep violet eyes shining. He knew Destiny would have loved it too.

Preeti smiled at him. She went over to the rabbit and guinea pig cages where there was a pile of old blankets, which she used to cover them at night. She shook out the cleanest one and brought it over.

'This will keep you warm,' she said, placing the blanket on Comet's back.

'Thank you, Preeti,' he neighed as she led him out of the barn.

Sounds of laughter and voices raised in greeting reached them. She caught a glimpse of jewel-bright saris through the lit-up windows. Viren was running excitedly up the garden towards the house.

'Everyone's here!' Preeti exclaimed excitedly. 'Come on, Comet, let's go and meet them.'

Comet had taken only a few steps, when he suddenly froze. Preeti heard a sound she'd been both hoping for and dreading.

The hollow sound of hooves galloping overhead.

'Destiny!'

Comet ran straight at the ranch-style

garden gate. He sailed over it and into
the alleyway, following the magical hoof-
beats, which sounded louder and closer.

Preeti ran after him. Her heart raced
as she opened the gate and flung herself
through it. She knew that this time
Comet was leaving for good and she was
going to have to be very strong and let
him go.

There was a violet flash and a twinkling
rainbow mist floated down around Comet.
He stood there in his true form, a grey-
brown pony no longer, but a magnificent
magic pony with a noble head, cream
coat and spreading gold-feathered wings.
His golden mane and tail flowed down in
shimmering silky strands.

'Comet!' Preeti gasped. She had almost
forgotten how beautiful he was. 'I . . . I

hope you catch Destiny. I'll never forget
you!' she said, her voice breaking.

Comet turned to look at her for one
last time, his eyes clouded with sadness.
'I will not forget you either. You have
been a good friend. Ride well and true,'

he said in a deep musical neigh.

There was a final flash of violet light and a silent burst of rainbow sparkles drifted down around Preeti in frozen snowflakes that tinkled as they hit the ground. Preeti gulped back tears, feeling as if her heart would break. She knew he would have to leave one day, but she couldn't believe it had happened so fast.

Something glittered in the snow. It was a single shimmering gold wing-feather. Reaching down, she picked it up. It tingled against her palm as it faded to a cream colour. She slipped it into her pocket, knowing she would treasure it always as a reminder of the wonderful adventure she had shared with the magic pony.

Then, as she turned and went back into

the garden, she saw Viren running towards her. 'I came to get you! Where's Comet?' he cried.

'His . . . his owner turned up and took him away in a horsebox,' Preeti said, wiping her eyes.

'Oh.' Viren's small face crumpled. 'I'm going to miss him loads.'

She put her arms round him, suddenly feeling like a grown-up big sister. It was a new feeling and she quite liked it. 'I know. Me too,' she said, wiping her eyes. 'But Comet never belonged to us, not really. We always knew he'd go back to the family who loved him as much as we did.' *The Lighting Herd on Rainbow Mist Island*, Preeti thought to herself sadly.

Viren nodded. 'But I wanted him to stay forever!'

'Me too,' Preeti said again gently. On impulse she bent and kissed his cheek.

'Yuck!' Viren scrubbed it away with his hand.

'Hey!' Preeti gave him a friendly nudge and he gave her a wobbly smile in return.

They walked towards the house hand in hand. Friends and relatives waved and

called to them. Laughter and singing floated out of the open door.

'Happy *Holi*! Happy *Holi*!'

The snow pony sparkled in the candlelight and seemed to turn towards Preeti and swish its tail. She felt herself smiling through her tears. *Take care, Comet. Thanks for being my friend. I hope you catch up with Destiny and take her home with you.*

Out Now

Magic Ponies

Could you be a little pony's special friend?

Magic Ponies

Pony Camp

SUE BENTLEY

Magic Ponies

A New Friend

A Special Wish

A Twinkle of Hooves

Showjumping Dreams

Seaside Summer

Riding Rescue

Winter Wonderland

Pony Camp

puffin.co.uk

Coming Soon

Could you be a little reindeer's special friend?

Magic Reindeer

A Christmas Wish

SUE BENTLEY

Magic Ponies

Win a Magic Ponies goody bag!

Golden feathers from Comet's wings are falling out as he desperately tries to find his twin sister, Destiny, who is still lost in our world! The feathers carry a secret message for Destiny.

Two words from the message can be found in magic golden feathers hidden in *Winter Wonderland* and *Pony Camp*.

To help save Destiny from danger, find the hidden words and put them together to complete the message. Send it in to us and each month we will put every correct message in a draw and pick out one lucky winner to receive a whole stable of Magic Ponies goodies!

Send your secret message, name and address on a postcard to:

Magic Ponies competition

Puffin Books

80 Strand

London WC2R 0RL

Please help Comet save his sister!

Good luck!

puffin.co.uk

It all started with a Scarecrow

Puffin is well over sixty years old.
Sounds ancient, doesn't it? But Puffin has never been
so lively. We're always on the lookout for the next big
idea, which is how it began all those years ago.

Penguin Books was a big idea from the mind of
a man called Allen Lane, who in 1935 invented
the quality paperback and changed the world.
**And from great Penguins, great Puffins grew,
changing the face of children's books forever.**

The first four Puffin Picture Books were hatched in 1940 and the
first Puffin story book featured a man with broomstick arms called
Worzel Gummidge. In 1967 Kaye Webb, Puffin Editor, started the
Puffin Club, promising to **'make children into readers'**.
She kept that promise and over 200,000 children became
devoted Puffineers through their quarterly instalments of
Puffin Post, which is now back for a new generation.

Many years from now, we hope you'll look back and
remember Puffin with a smile. **No matter what your age
or what you're into, there's a Puffin for everyone.**
The possibilities are endless, but one thing is for sure:
whether it's a picture book or a paperback, a sticker book
or a hardback, **if it's got that little Puffin
on it – it's bound to be good.**